A Christopher Ranch Story

Elephant Garlic

– **Written by** –

Ken Christopher

– **Illustrated by** –   – **Designed by** –

Danny Voight   Articulate Solutions, Inc.

MEDIUS

Printed by Medius Corporation

Today is a very important day—
a celebration of every animal's favorite food!

Dearest Friend,

At a quarter to two today, we will all gather to enjoy a marvelous feast.

It is kindly requested, or rather suggested, you bring your favorite food.

The King

The elephant sighs and shakes his head,
surely a decision he's come to dread:
How to decide one's favorite food?

With so much fresh produce
from which to choose,
surely his friends can help him peruse.

"Oh look, it's Mr. Mouse!"

"Mr. Mouse, Mr. Mouse,
a quarter to two today
is not so far away.
Perhaps I'll bring some cheese."

"Oh, silly Elephant, everyone knows
that cheese and mice are just how it goes.
The cheese is *mine* to bring."

"Oh look, it's Mr. Rabbit!"

"Mr. Rabbit, Mr. Rabbit,
a quarter to two today
is coming right our way.
Perhaps I'll bring a carrot!"

"Oh, funny Elephant, everyone knows
that carrots and rabbits are just how it goes.
The carrot is *mine* to bring."

"Oh look, it's Mrs. Bear!"

"Mrs. Bear, Mrs. Bear,
A quarter to two today
is approaching to my dismay.
Perhaps I'll bring some honey."

"Oh little Elephant, everyone knows
that honey and bears are just how it goes.
The honey is *mine* to bring."

"Oh look, it's Mr. Monkey!"

"Mr. Monkey, Mr. Monkey,
 A quarter to two today
 mustn't be delayed.
 Perhaps I'll bring bananas."

"Oh fussy Elephant, everyone knows
that bananas and monkeys are just how it goes.
Bananas are *mine* to bring."

The clock rang
at a quarter to two,
and the poor little elephant
didn't know what to do...

He tried cheese to no avail,
and at carrots, he felt he failed.
Even honey and bananas
weren't right for him.

"Mr. Elephant, Mr. Elephant, all is not lost.
You tried and you stumbled, but not at all costs."

"Look to my garden,
    as something will be found.
    If you close your eyes and believe
    in yourself, it may be underground."

The elephant took a breath, reached out
his trunk, and wrapped it around a stem.
With all his might he pulled really tight,
and found something just for him.

"You've done it Mr. Elephant,
you've done your best!
A supremely large garlic,
bigger than the rest."

"This perfect addition
to our friendship stew
now and forever will be
named after you."

"Listen, listen, I've something to say...
Elephant Garlic is here to stay!"

At a quarter past nine,
just past his bed time,
the elephant slumbered away
content that he at last
found his favorite food.